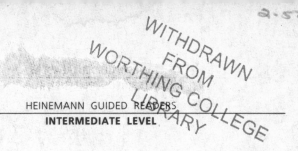

HEINEMANN GUIDED READERS
INTERMEDIATE LEVEL

JOSEPHINE TEY

The Franchise Affair

Retold by Margaret Tarner

D1627894

HEINEMANN

Series Editor: John Milne

The Heinemann Guided Readers provide a choice of enjoyable reading material for learners of English. The series is published at five levels – Starter, Beginner, Elementary, Intermediate and Upper. At **Intermediate Level**, the control of content and language has the following main features:

Information Control

Information which is vital to the understanding of the story is presented in an easily assimilated manner and is repeated when necessary. Difficult allusion and metaphor are avoided and cultural backgrounds are made explicit.

Structure Control

Most of the structures used in the Readers will be familiar to students who have completed an elementary course of English. Other grammatical features may occur, but their use is made clear through context and reinforcement. This ensures that the reading, as well as being enjoyable, provides a continual learning situation for the students. Sentences are limited in most cases to a maximum of three clauses and within sentences there is a balanced use of adverbial and adjectival phrases. Great care is taken with pronoun reference.

Vocabulary Control

There is a basic vocabulary of approximately 1,600 words. Help is given to the students in the form of illustrations, which are closely related to the text.

Glossary

Some difficult words and phrases in this book are important for understanding the story. Some of these words are explained in the story, some are shown in the pictures, and others are marked with a number like this . . .³ Words with a number are explained in the Glossary on page 59.

Contents

	A Note About the People in This Story	4
1	The Franchise	6
2	Betty Kane's Story	9
3	*The Morning Watch*	14
4	Robert Asks Some Questions	18
5	The Girl in the Brown Hat	22
6	'There's Still Hope'	26
7	A Summons to Appear in Court	28
8	New Evidence	30
9	Kevin Visits The Franchise	33
10	The Magistrate's Court	35
11	Mr Lange	39
12	The Trial	43
13	The Truth	47
14	The End of the Franchise Affair	50
	Points for Understanding	53
	Glossary	59
	List of titles at Intermediate Level	63

A Note About the People in This Story

Marion Sharpe lives with her old mother, **Mrs Sharpe**, outside the town of Milford. Their house is old and white, with a high wall around it. The house is called The Franchise.

Robert Blair is a solicitor. He lives in Milford with his **Aunt Lin**. He works in the town of Milford.

Betty Kane is fifteen. Her parents are dead. She lives with her guardian, **Mrs Wynn**, in Aylesbury, near London. Mrs Wynn has a son, **Leslie**.

Kevin Macdermott is a barrister. He lives and works in London. **Alec Ramsden** is a private detective. He works for Robert Blair and Kevin Macdermott.

Detective-Inspector Grant is a policeman from Scotland Yard in London. He has come from London to help **Inspector Hallam** of the Milford police with an important case.

Rose Glyn worked as a servant for the Sharpes in The Franchise. **Gladys Rees** is Rose Glyn's friend.

Bernard Chadwick is a businessman. He often travels abroad. **Frances Chadwick** is Bernard Chadwick's wife.

Mrs Tilset is Betty Kane's aunt. She lives in Larborough. **Mr Lange** is Danish. He owns The Red Shoes Hotel in Copenhagen, Denmark.

1

The Franchise

It was four o'clock on a spring afternoon. Robert Blair was sitting at his office desk.

Robert Blair was a solicitor[1]. He was forty years old. He had lived and worked in the little town of Milford all his life. Robert was not married. He lived with his Aunt Lin in a house in the High Street.

It was time to go home. Robert stood up. At that moment, the telephone rang. Robert answered it. And his life changed forever.

'Is that Mr Blair?' a woman's voice asked. 'You don't know me, Mr Blair. My name's Marion Sharpe. I live with my mother at The Franchise. That's the big house on the Larborough road.'

'Yes, I know it,' Robert Blair said. 'It's on the road between Milford and Larborough.'

The woman's deep voice went on.

'I'm in trouble, Mr Blair,' said the woman. 'I need a solicitor. There's a policeman here – from Scotland Yard[2]. He says my mother and I kidnapped[3] someone and kept her here, in The Franchise . . .'

'Kidnapped?' Robert said in surprise.

'I can't tell you on the phone,' Marion Sharpe said quickly. 'Can you come out here straightaway? There's been a mistake. I'm sure you will be able to help me.'

Ten minutes later, Robert was driving out of Milford. Old Mrs Sharpe and her daughter had lived in The Franchise for three or four years. They did their shopping in Milford, but they had no friends there. Many people in Milford thought that the Sharpes were strange and unusual.

Marion Sharpe was a tall, slim, forty-year old woman. She had

'I'm in trouble, Mr Blair. I need a solicitor.'

a sun-tanned face and she usually wore a brightly-coloured scarf round her neck.

Her mother, old Mrs Sharpe, had white hair. Robert had seen her in Milford, sitting in the back of their old grey car.

The Franchise was an old house. It stood two miles outside Milford on the Larborough road. The house had a high wall all round it. The high iron gates were always closed.

When Robert arrived, there were two cars outside the gates. One car belonged to the police inspector of Milford. There were three people sitting in the other car. There was the driver, and in the back, a policewoman and a young girl.

Robert pushed open the heavy iron gates. The big white house was old and rather ugly. The front door was opened by Marion Sharpe.

'Thank you for coming so quickly,' she said.

Two men and a woman were in the sitting-room. Robert knew Inspector Hallam well. He was the police inspector at Milford. Mrs Sharpe, a white-haired old woman, was sitting very straight in her chair.

'This is Detective-Inspector Grant from Scotland Yard,' said Marion Sharpe introducing the second man. 'Detective-Inspector Grant thinks my mother and I kidnapped a young girl three weeks ago. The girl says we brought her here, starved[4] her and beat her.'

2

Betty Kane's Story

Detective-Inspector Grant opened his notebook and began to speak.

'Betty Kane is a schoolgirl. She is fifteen years old – nearly sixteen. Her parents were killed in the war. She now lives with her guardian, Mrs Wynn, in Aylesbury, near London.

'Betty Kane went to spend her Easter holidays with her aunt, in Larborough,' went on Grant. 'Her aunt is called Mrs Tilset. She was going to stay there for a week.

'But after a week, Betty Kane sent Mrs Wynn a postcard. She said she was going to stay in Larborough with her aunt for the rest of her school holiday.'

'How long was that?' Robert Blair asked.

'Another three weeks,' Grant replied. 'But after three weeks, Betty Kane did not come home. So Mrs Wynn wrote to Mrs Tilset in Larborough and asked her to send Betty home.'

'Why didn't Mrs Wynn phone?'

'Because Mrs Tilset, Betty's aunt, hasn't got a phone,' Grant explained. 'Mrs Tilset wrote back to say that Betty had left Larborough on 28th March. By the time the police were told, Betty Kane had been missing for more than three weeks.

'A few days after the police were told, Betty Kane came home. She was wearing only a thin dress and shoes. It was very cold, but she had no coat. She was covered with bruises[5].'

'What did she tell her guardian?' asked Robert Blair.

'Betty Kane said she had been locked up in an attic[6], beaten and starved. She said two women had brought her to this house in their car.'

Marion Sharpe laughed.

'The girl described our car!' she said.

9

'She also described this house,' said Grant. 'And Miss Sharpe and her mother.'

'How did the girl get here?' Robert asked.

'Betty Kane was waiting in Larborough for the bus to go home to Aylesbury,' Grant explained. 'A car stopped. The woman who was driving told Betty that she had missed the bus. It had gone earlier. The woman offered Betty a lift[7] to another bus stop to catch a different bus. It was raining and getting dark, so Betty got into the car. But after some time, the car stopped outside a big house. It had a high wall round it.

'The woman invited the girl to go in and have something to eat and drink. But the coffee had something in it that made the girl sleep. Betty Kane woke up the following morning in a small attic with a round window.'

'A round window?' Robert Blair repeated.

'Yes,' said Marion Sharpe. 'There's a round window in our attic. The girl said we wanted her to be our maid. She also said we starved and beat her when she refused. She told the police we took away all her clothes except a dress. And we locked her in.'

'Then how did the girl get away?' Robert Blair asked.

'One evening, the younger woman forgot to lock the door,' Grant said. 'The girl ran down the stairs and out of the house. A lorry driver gave her a lift to Aylesbury. She arrived home completely exhausted[8], just after midnight.'

There was silence in the room. Old Mrs Sharpe moved angrily in her chair, but she said nothing.

'Why is the girl so sure that this was the house?' Robert Blair asked. 'It was dark when the car stopped.'

'Betty Kane says they passed a bus with "Milford" written on it.'

Grant looked down at his notebook. Betty Kane's statement was written in the notebook. Grant read out what Betty Kane had told the police: ' "From the window of the attic, I could see a high brick wall and big iron gates. Inside the gates, the drive[9] went

10

straight and then divided into two, to make a circle." '

Grant shut his notebook and looked up.

'There is only one house like that near Milford – this house,' he said. 'I've brought Betty Kane here to check some details[10].'

Detective-Inspector Grant left the room. When the door opened, Marion Sharpe stood up slowly. Mrs Sharpe sat completely still.

The girl was wearing her school coat and shoes. She was not beautiful. But she had pretty, dark brown eyes. She looked calmly at Marion Sharpe and then at Mrs Sharpe.

Why has this girl told this strange story? Robert Blair thought. What would this girl look like if she was wearing grown-up clothes and had make-up on her face?

'Are these the women?' Detective-Inspector Grant asked the girl.

'Yes, those are the women,' Betty Kane said in a quiet voice. 'They kept me here and beat me.'

'The girl's a good liar[11],' Mrs Sharpe said. 'What are you going to do now, Detective-Inspector? Arrest[12] us?'

'I want to take Miss Kane to the attic. I want to check the details of her statement.'

'I see.' The old lady stood up.

'I usually have a rest in the afternoon, Detective-Inspector. I am going to rest now,' she said. She moved towards the door. Betty Kane took a step back. For the first time, she looked afraid.

Mrs Sharpe stared at the girl.

'I am sure you will recognise[13] our attic,' she said. 'I shall see you again before the end of this affair[14], Miss Kane. Goodbye, Mr Blair, and thank you for coming.'

The door closed behind the old woman.

'I'll read what Betty Kane said about the attic,' Detective-Inspector Grant said. He opened his notebook again.

' "The attic was square, with a bed and a wooden chair.

11

'. . . those are the women. They kept me here and beat me.'

The younger woman took the chair away when I tried to break the window with it." '

When they reached the attic, it was empty. But Robert could see the marks where there had been a bed. And there was a crack in the round window.

'There were two suitcases here too,' Betty Kane said. 'One was brown leather with dark corners. The other one had stripes.'

'Can we see your suitcases, Miss Sharpe?' Grant asked. Marion led them to a cupboard. As Marion opened the cupboard door, Robert looked at Betty Kane. For a second, he saw a smile on the girl's face.

In the cupboard were two suitcases – one brown and the other striped.

They went next to the garage at the back of the house. Detective-Inspector Grant read from his notebook again.

' "The car was old and grey. One front wheel was a lighter colour than the others." '

The Sharpes' car was old and grey. One front wheel was a lighter colour than the others.

'Thank you very much, Miss Sharpe,' Grant said at last. 'I shall be phoning you in the next few days.'

The police and the girl left. Robert Blair returned to the house with Marion Sharpe.

'I don't understand it, do you?' Marion Sharpe said. 'How did the girl know these things?'

'She didn't know, she guessed,' Robert said. 'Lots of people have suitcases like yours. She guessed correctly. If your suitcases had been different, she could have said that you had thrown the other suitcases away.'

'But how did she know about the car?' Marion asked. 'And she described my mother and me so clearly. She told the police she had never been to Milford.'

'That's what she said,' Robert answered. 'But she must have been there. Or perhaps she saw you outside The Franchise.'

'There's one thing I am sure about,' Marion said. 'During the time she was away, Betty Kane did something that she wants to hide. And she was with someone. Someone who beat her. She was probably with a man. I'm glad he beat her. A girl who tells such lies should be beaten.

'What will happen to us if the police believe this girl's story?'

'I'm not sure,' Robert answered. 'But you could both be sent to prison.'

'Then you must find out the truth, Mr Blair.'

3

The Morning Watch

A week later, Robert phoned Marion Sharpe. He had some very good news for the Sharpes. Scotland Yard had told him that they were going to do nothing more about the case[15].

Robert arranged to meet the Sharpes the next day in his office at twelve o'clock.

In the past week, Robert had thought a lot about Marion Sharpe. She was an interesting and unusual woman.

Robert decided that he would find out the truth about Betty Kane. He would find out where she had been. He would solve[16] The Franchise Affair himself. It was clear that the police were not going to do anything more about it.

But on the Friday morning, Robert had an unpleasant surprise. Betty Kane's story filled the front page of the newspaper, *The Morning Watch*.

Above a big photograph of Betty Kane was the headline, THIS IS THE GIRL. Below it, was a smaller photograph of The

14

Franchise with the headline: IS THIS THE HOUSE?

Robert looked at the paper as he sat in his office. Every word of Betty Kane's story was written there. *The Morning Watch* believed her story. And the police were asked why they had not arrested the two women.

At twelve o'clock, the Sharpes arrived in Robert's office.

'People have been looking at us very strangely this morning,' Marion said. 'We went into a café to have coffee, but they told us there was no room!'

'They've read this,' Robert said quietly, pointing to the newspaper on his desk.

'Oh, no!' said Marion looking at the front page of *The Morning Watch*. 'Now everyone will believe this girl's story. And there's nothing we can do!'

'Oh yes, there is something we can do,' said Robert quickly. 'First, we know that Betty Kane was never at The Franchise.'

'Well, we know it, but do you?' Marion asked.

'Yes, I do,' Robert replied.

'Thank you for believing us, Mr Blair,' Marion said with a smile. 'But how did the girl see the house? The walls are high and the gates are always shut.'

'Could she have seen over the walls from a bus?' asked Robert.

'Buses pass the house on the way to Milford,' said Marion, 'but they are not double-deckers. And a passenger on a single-decker bus could not see over the walls.'

'She saw the house somehow,' Robert said. 'But we must find out where she was. This photograph of her in *The Morning Watch* may help us. Someone may see it and recognise her.

'I'm going to talk to people who know Betty Kane,' Robert went on. 'I want to find out what she's really like. Then I may be able to find out what she did.'

'Where will you start, Mr Blair?' Marion Sharpe asked.

'At her home,' Robert replied. 'I'm leaving for Aylesbury after lunch.'

'We are very grateful to you,' old Mrs Sharpe said.

———

A few hours later, Robert was standing outside 39 Meadowside Lane, Aylesbury. There were pretty flowers in the small garden in front of the house.

Mrs Wynn, Betty Kane's guardian, was a small, pretty woman. Her brown eyes were bright and intelligent.

Robert explained why he was there.

'I'm afraid Betty isn't here,' Mrs Wynn said. 'She's away for the day with my son, Leslie. It was Leslie who told the newspaper about what happened to Betty. He was so angry that the police were doing nothing.'

'Are Betty and Leslie good friends?' Robert Blair asked Mrs Wynn.

'Oh yes,' said Mrs Wynn. 'They were very good friends. Until Leslie got engaged[17], Leslie and Betty did everything together.'

'What did Betty say when Leslie got engaged?' Robert asked quickly.

Mrs Wynn smiled. 'She wasn't jealous[18], Mr Blair,' she said. 'Betty is a very nice girl, truthful and hard-working. But now she's nearly sixteen, she's getting rather bored with school. I expect she'll get married young, as I did.'

'You say Betty is truthful, Mrs Wynn,' Robert said. 'Do you believe what she told you about the weeks she was missing?'

'Of course. How could she invent[19] a story like that?'

'Betty was ill when she first came home, wasn't she?' said Robert. 'Perhaps she forgot some of the details.'

'Oh, no,' Mrs Wynn said. 'Betty never forgets anything she has seen. She's got a photographic memory[20].'

16

'Betty never forgets anything she has seen. She's got a
photographic memory.'

'Then perhaps she sometimes made up stories?' asked Robert.

Mrs Wynn smiled again. 'Betty never invents things.'

'Well, thank you, Mrs Wynn,' said Robert Blair. 'You have been very helpful. If you ever think of anything strange about Betty's story, please let me know.'

'I'm sure I won't, Mr Blair,' Mrs Wynn said quickly.

But Robert did notice that Mrs Wynn looked worried for a moment. Without thinking, he said, 'Did Betty have anything in her pockets when she came home?'

Mrs Wynn didn't answer at once. Then she said, 'There was a lipstick in a gold case in the pocket of her dress. That's all.'

Robert said goodbye and got into his car. As he drove away, he thought about Betty Kane. She had a photographic memory – she could remember details of things she had only seen once. She was bored with school. And she had come home with a gold lipstick case in her pocket.

Robert smiled. Betty Kane was hiding something. And Robert was going to find out what it was!

4

Robert Asks Some Questions

Robert drove on to London. He had arranged to meet an old friend, Kevin Macdermott.

Kevin Macdermott was a very clever barrister[21]. Robert wanted to talk to him about The Franchise Affair and to ask him for his opinion[22].

Robert told Kevin Macdermott everything about The Franchise Affair and about the Sharpes. Macdermott listened carefully.

'So that's the story,' Robert said at last. 'It's clear that the girl is lying.'

'No!' said Kevin. 'I can believe every word of the Kane girl's story . . .'

'But, Kevin!' Robert cried.

Kevin smiled.

'And, I can also believe that Betty Kane is a very clever liar! That's my job. I'm a barrister. That means I can see both sides of a question. In my opinion, if the girl was in court, most people would believe her, not the Sharpes.'

After a moment, Kevin added quietly, 'I wonder where Betty Kane was all those weeks she was away? The girl interests me. Her story is so strange. She tells it so carefully . . .'

'Do you think the police believe her story?' Robert asked.

'If the police get just one piece of evidence against the Sharpes,' said Kevin, 'they will arrest them at once.'

'They won't find anything against the Sharpes,' said Robert. 'And I am going to show that Betty Kane is lying. Tomorrow I'm going to Larborough. I am going to talk to Betty's aunt, Mrs Tilset. I will find out something about the girl. She was with someone during those weeks. Someone must know where she was.'

———

The following afternoon, Robert stopped his car outside 93 Cherill Street in Larborough.

A few minutes later, Robert was drinking tea in Mrs Tilset's little sitting-room. It was a dull little room and Mrs Tilset was a dull little woman. Why had Betty Kane enjoyed staying with her?

Mrs Tilset was a dull woman. Why had Betty enjoyed staying with her?

'Did Betty make any friends when she was here?' Robert asked.

'Friends? Oh no. Betty spent most of her time in the cinema. There are plenty of cinemas here in Larborough.'

'She went to the cinema every afternoon?' Robert asked in surprise.

'No, she went every morning. The cinemas are cheaper before twelve o'clock. Then she went on a bus somewhere. She travelled all around.'

'So she was out all day?'

'That's right. But she was usually home by six-thirty or seven. I always had supper ready for her.'

So Betty Kane had been on her own, every day, for a fortnight!

'You told the police that Betty was on her own?' Robert asked quietly.

'Well, yes . . .' Mrs Tilset said slowly. Then she said, 'They asked me if I went out with her sometimes and I said I did. But there was nothing wrong in Betty being out alone, was there?'

'Did Betty ever go to Milford – on a bus?' asked Robert.

'I don't know,' Mrs Tilset replied. 'The police asked me that. You're not from the police, are you?'

'No, Mrs Tilset,' Robert said slowly. 'I told you I was a solicitor. And I told you I'm representing the Sharpes.'

'Oh, yes. They're the two women who kept Betty in their house, aren't they?' said Mrs Tilset. 'How could they beat a poor girl like that! She was lucky to escape, wasn't she?'

But Robert stood up to go. It was clear that he would not get any facts from Mrs Tilset.

Before leaving Larborough, Robert drove to the bus station and asked a few questions there. After that, he drove back to Milford.

5

The Girl in the Brown Hat

The next day was Sunday and Robert drove out to The Franchise. Marion and Mrs Sharpe were very pleased to see him.

Robert told the Sharpes about his visit to Mrs Tilset. Then he said, 'But I have something more interesting to tell you. I've found out how Betty Kane saw over the wall into The Franchise. You know that the buses which go from Milford to Larborough pass by here?'

'Yes,' said Marion. 'But they are usually single-decker buses. You can't see into The Franchise from a single-decker bus.'

'Yes, I agree,' said Robert. 'But I went to the bus station at Milford last night. And I was told that twice they used double-decker buses during the time Betty Kane went to Larborough.'

Marion looked excited.

'So that's how she saw over the wall!'

'Yes,' Robert said. 'I'm sure that she saw you, the house and the car, from the bus. And she saw the drive, the round window – everything! The girl has a photographic memory, you know, so she remembered every detail. And buses on country roads go slowly.'

'Do we tell the police about this?' Mrs Sharpe asked.

'No,' Robert answered. 'I'm afraid it doesn't prove anything. She just remembered what she saw and used it. We still don't know what she was doing all that time. But I think she met someone in Larborough. Now I've got to find out who she met!'

'Mr Blair,' old Mrs Sharpe said. 'You have spent a lot of time finding out these things. But you have your own work to do. You're not a private detective[23].'

'But I'm enjoying being a detective,' Robert said with a smile. 'And Larborough isn't far away from Milford.'

'What do you plan to do now?' Marion asked.

'Well, we know Betty Kane had lunch somewhere. So I'm going to all the coffee-shops in Larborough with her photograph. Someone is sure to recognise her. Perhaps one of the bus drivers will remember her.'

'Well, Mr Blair, we must thank you for all the help you are giving us,' Mrs Sharpe said. 'Good luck!'

———

Robert spent Monday morning drinking coffee in Larborough. By half past twelve, he had visited all the coffee-shops, but he found out nothing. No one remembered Betty Kane.

Robert felt tired. He walked into the Midland Hotel to have a drink. The waiter in the hotel knew Robert well.

Robert took out his copy of *The Morning Watch* and looked at the photograph of Betty Kane again.

'Have you ever seen this girl in here, Albert?' Robert asked the waiter.

'No, sir. Young girls cannot come in the hotel lounge.'

'If she had a hat on she might look older,' Robert said slowly.

'A hat!' the waiter repeated. 'Wait a minute, I *have* seen her! She's the girl in the brown hat! That's why I noticed her. She wore the same clothes every day – a blue dress, a brown hat and a brown coat.'

'Did she come here alone?' Robert asked the waiter.

'Yes, at first,' the waiter replied, 'Then one day, she started talking to a young man at the next table.'

'You mean he started talking to her,' Robert said smiling.

'Oh, no, she started talking first,' the waiter replied. 'Then she sat at the young man's table. Soon the two of them were talking to each other like old friends!'

'. . . one day, she started talking to a young man . . .'

'Did you know the man? What did he look like?'

'No, sir, I'd never seen him before,' the waiter replied. 'He was young and had dark hair. That's all I remember.'

————

On the way home, Robert stopped at The Franchise. He was surprised to see a policeman standing outside the iron gates. The policeman let Robert in.

'I'm pleased that you have come,' Marion said. 'Before the policeman came, there were people sitting on the wall shouting at us. And we've had people phoning us saying really horrible things.'

'It is that newspaper – *The Morning Watch*,' said Robert. 'They have written more about Betty. They are making people angry. They are saying that she is such a good girl. But listen to what I have found out. She is not such a good girl at all.'

And Robert told the Sharpes what he had found out from the waiter in the Midland Hotel.

'I'm going to prove that Betty Kane is a liar,' said Robert. 'I'll come and see you again tomorrow.'

He stood up, then asked, 'Is the policeman going to stay here all night?'

'No, I'm afraid not,' Marion answered. 'But I don't think people will come here at night.'

But Marion was wrong.

At midnight, the phone rang in Robert's house. Half-asleep, Robert answered it.

'It's Marion Sharpe,' a voice said quickly. 'Some people have climbed over the wall. I think they're . . .' There was the sound of breaking glass. Then there was silence. Robert put down the phone and then phoned the police.

'Miss Sharpe has already phoned us,' a voice said. 'A police car is on its way there now.'

The gates of The Franchise were wide open when Robert arrived. There were lights on in the downstairs rooms. Many of the windows were broken.

Inside the front room, there were bricks and broken bottles lying on the floor and the furniture.

Mrs Sharpe came into the room carrying a coffee-pot.

'Ah, Mr Blair. Thank you for coming. We didn't know if you got our message. They have cut the telephone wires.'

'You must leave The Franchise,' Robert said. 'It's too dangerous to stay here now. You must go and stay in a hotel in Larborough.'

'Certainly not,' said Mrs Sharpe. 'Look what they have done while we are here. What do you think would happen to The Franchise if it was left empty? No, Mr Blair, this is our home and we are staying here!'

6

'There's Still Hope'

It was Tuesday afternoon. Two weeks ago, Robert Blair had thought that life was boring. And then Marion Sharpe had phoned and everything had changed. Robert had never before been so busy – or so happy.

Robert was pleased. He had had the broken windows at The Franchise repaired. A strong lock had been fitted to the gate. That morning, Robert had taken some food to The Franchise. And some flowers for Marion Sharpe.

Marion had been surprised by the flowers. She had smiled happily. Robert had never met anyone like Marion before. He liked her very much.

That evening, Robert phoned Kevin Macdermott.

'The young man who met Betty Kane in the Midland Hotel must be found at once,' Robert told the barrister.

'So you need the name of a private detective, do you?' Kevin said.

'But surely the police will look for the man!' Robert said in surprise.

'No, they won't,' Kevin answered. 'That is not their job. If the police think Betty Kane is lying, they won't do any more work on the case.'

'But what about the Sharpes? People will still think they are guilty[24]. I want their name to be cleared[25].'

'If you want the Sharpes' name cleared, you need a private detective,' said Kevin Macdermott. 'I know a good detective. His name's Alec Ramsden. Let me give you his phone number.'

———

Alec Ramsden was in Robert's office early the following morning. Robert gave him a copy of Betty Kane's statement. Then he told Ramsden everything he had found out. Lastly, he told him about the young man in the Midland Hotel.

'Your job is to find that young man,' Robert said, 'and find him as soon as you can.'

'Right, I'll start looking straightaway, Mr Blair,' Ramsden said.

After Alec Ramsden left, Robert went to the Rose and Crown for a cup of coffee. Robert took a seat near a window and looked out at the busy street. Suddenly he saw the Sharpes' old grey car! Why had they come into Milford?

Robert left the Rose and Crown and walked quickly down the little street. He reached the car as Marion Sharpe got out.

'Miss Sharpe,' he said quietly, 'why are you here? You must know how silly it is.'

'It may be silly, but we had to come. We can't hide all the time. Mother and I are going to a café. The people at Milford must get used to seeing us again. Then they may stop talking about us.'

'They will talk even more,' said Robert. 'Please, Miss Sharpe, drive your car to the Rose and Crown. Have coffee with me there.'

'Very well, Mr Blair,' Marion said. 'You are right. Get in and we can drive there together.'

Robert sat next to Marion. Everyone was staring at the little car. But Marion smiled at Robert and he felt happy.

In the Rose and Crown, Robert told the Sharpes about Alec Ramsden.

'If anyone can find out the truth about Betty Kane, he will,' Robert told them.

'No one has recognised her from that photograph, have they?' asked Marion. 'I wonder why. It was in the newspaper five days ago.'

'Someone may not have seen that newspaper yet,' Robert said. 'There's still hope. People sometimes keep newspapers and look at them weeks later.'

7

A Summons to Appear in Court

On Friday, Robert was in his office. He had eaten a good lunch and he felt happy.

Then the phone rang.

'Mr Blair? This is Inspector Hallam of the Milford police. I have bad news for you, I'm afraid. Detective-Inspector Grant from Scotland Yard is here. And he has brought a summons for the Sharpes to appear in court[26].'

'I don't believe it!' said Robert.

'The police have found two witnesses[27]. They'll prove that Betty Kane's story is true,' Hallam said.

Robert hurried to the police station.

'What new evidence[28] have you found?' Robert asked Detective-Inspector Grant.

'We have a man who saw Betty Kane at the bus stop. He saw her getting into the car.'

'Into *a* car,' said Robert. 'There are thousands of cars like the Sharpes'.'

'And we have found a girl,' Grant said quietly. 'She used to work for the Sharpes. Her name is Rose Glyn. She says she heard screams coming from the attic in The Franchise. And she told her friend, Gladys Rees, about it.'

'But that is not evidence,' said Robert. 'She must have read about the case in the newspaper. Then she told her friend about the screams.'

'No, not at all,' said Detective-Inspsector Grant. 'She told her friend before the case was in the newspaper.'

'When do you want the Sharpes to appear in court?' asked Robert.

'On Monday,' replied Detective-Inspector Grant. 'I'll be in court on Monday, Mr Blair.

'Hallam will go with you now to The Franchise. He will give the Sharpes the summons to appear in court.'

Robert and Inspector Hallam drove to The Franchise. Marion Sharpe opened the door.

'How nice to see you –' Marion began. Then she saw Inspector Hallam's face. The Inspector was not smiling.

'Good afternoon, Miss Sharpe,' the Inspector said politely. 'I'm afraid I must speak to you and your mother.'

At that moment, old Mrs Sharpe walked into the room. She looked at Inspector Hallam in surprise.

'What is it now, Inspector?' she asked.

'I'm afraid I've come with a summons,' the Inspector said quietly.

'A summons?' Marion repeated.

'A summons to appear in court on Monday morning. You are both charged with abduction and assault[29]. With keeping Betty Kane here and beating her.'

'I don't believe it,' Marion said slowly. She turned to Robert. 'Why have the police decided to charge us now?'

'The police have new evidence,' Robert said unhappily. 'You'll have to take the summons. We can talk about it when the Inspector has gone.'

8

New Evidence

'What is this new evidence?' Mrs Sharpe asked Robert. Robert told them about the witness who had seen Betty Kane get into a car at the bus stop. Then he said, 'But that is not very important. The other evidence is more important. Did you have a girl called Rose Glyn working for you here at The Franchise?'

'Yes, we did. But we sacked[30] her. That happened before the police brought Betty Kane to this house.'

'Why did you sack her?'

'For stealing,' said old Mrs Sharpe. 'She stole money, anything she could.'

'And then she stole a watch I'd had for twenty years,' said Marion. 'We couldn't prove she'd stolen it, but we knew she had. So we went to the girl's home and told her not to come back. And that same afternoon, the police came here, with Betty Kane.'

There was a short silence and then Robert said, 'Rose Glyn will swear[31] in court that she heard screams coming from your attic. And she will swear that she told her friend before anyone had heard of Betty Kane.'

'That is a problem,' said Marion. 'And it is your problem as well as our problem. You may think now that we have been lying to you.'

'Nonsense, Marion,' Robert said. Neither of them noticed that he had called her Marion for the first time. 'I know who is lying. It is Betty Kane. And we will prove in court that she is a liar.'

'Will we be able to prove that she is a liar?' asked Marion.

'Yes, I am sure,' Robert said firmly. 'I believe what you told me is true. I don't know how we will prove that Betty Kane is lying. But I am sure we will.'

'What happens now?' asked Marion.

'You will both have to go to the Magistrate's Court[32] on Monday morning,' said Robert. 'You will both plead not guilty. You will be sent for trial at the Assizes. I will arrange bail for you. And you can stay here at The Franchise until the trial.'

———

Late that evening, Alec Ramsden phoned Robert at home. He had nothing to report. The young man the waiter had seen talking to Betty Kane had never stayed at the Midland Hotel. No one recognised the photograph of Betty Kane at any railway station or airport.

Robert told Alec Ramsden about the new evidence and the summons.

'It is very important now,' said Robert, 'that you find the young man.'

Robert then phoned Kevin Macdermott. He needed his help. Kevin agreed to come down to Milford and meet the Sharpes at the weekend.

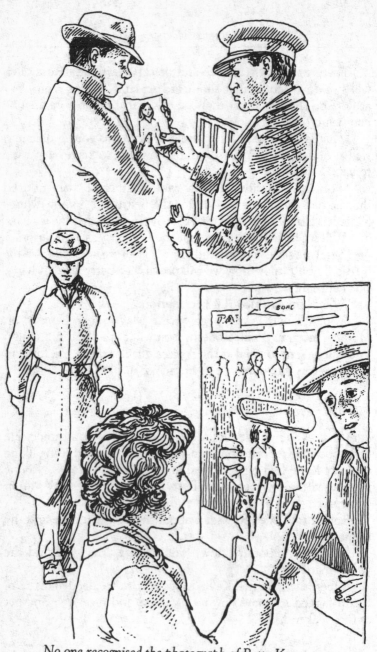

No one recognised the photograph of Betty Kane . . .

9

Kevin Visits The Franchise

Kevin Macdermott arrived in Milford on Saturday evening. On Sunday morning, the two men drove out to The Franchise. Robert took Betty Kane's statement with him as Marion had asked him to. Robert introduced Kevin to old Mrs Sharpe and to Marion.

'Let's have some coffee,' said Marion. 'Then I want to take you and Mr Macdermott up to the attic. I think Betty Kane made a mistake in her statement. It may be very important.'

After coffee they walked upstairs to the attic. Kevin Macdermott looked round the small room.

'So this is the room where Betty Kane said she was kept a prisoner,' he said quietly. He walked over to the round window and looked out.

Then he turned to Marion and asked, 'What mistake has Betty Kane made in her statement?'

'Have you got Betty Kane's statement there, Mr Blair?' Marion asked Robert. 'Will you read out the part where she says what she could see from the window?'

Robert began to read: ' "From the window of the attic, I could see a high brick wall with big iron gates. Inside the gates, the drive went straight and then divided into two to make a circle. I . . ." '

'Stop!' Kevin shouted. 'Read that last bit again, Robert!'

' "The drive went straight and then divided . . ." '

Robert stopped as Kevin gave a shout of laughter.

'You see?' said Marion.

'See what?' Robert asked. He walked over to the window and then he understood. From this window, you could not see that the drive made a circle!

' "The drive went straight and then divided . . ." '

'Do you think this is enough to prove Betty Kane is lying?' asked Marion quickly.

'No, I'm afraid not,' Kevin replied. 'She can say she saw the circle of the drive in the car's headlights. Don't speak about this in court tomorrow, Robert.

'In fact,' Kevin went on, 'keep everything as simple as possible in court tomorrow. Get bail for Miss Sharpe and her mother.'

'And, by the time the trial comes up at the Assizes,' said Robert, 'I will have enough evidence to prove that Betty Kane is lying.'

10

The Magistrate's Court

On Monday, the Magistrate's Court was very crowded. The Franchise Affair was the most exciting thing that had happened in Milford for years. Everybody wanted to be in the courtroom.

The Sharpes stood side by side in the dock[33]. Both women looked tired.

And then Robert saw Betty Kane.

She was wearing a pale grey dress. Her face looked young and innocent[34]. As she walked to the witness box, everyone in the courtroom watched her.

But this girl is not innocent, Robert thought to himself. She went away and stayed with a man. I'm sure that's what she did. But who will believe it?

Betty Kane told her story in a clear, sweet voice.

'Are these the two women who beat you and kept you prisoner in their house?' the Magistrate asked.

Betty Kane looked at the Sharpes.

'Yes,' she answered quietly.

35

Her face looked young and innocent.

'Mr Blair,' the Magistrate asked, 'do you want to ask Miss Kane any questions?'

'No, sir. I have no questions,' Robert answered.

Then the witnesses were called. First, the man who had seen Betty Kane get into the car at the bus stop. Yes, he had seen the car clearly, but he hadn't noticed the number.

Next came Rose Glyn, the girl who had worked for the Sharpes.

Rose Glyn was wearing a brightly-coloured dress and a hat with flowers on it. She smiled at everyone in court except the Sharpes.

Rose said she had heard screams coming from the Sharpes' attic on Monday 15th April. She was frightened and decided not to work for the Sharpes any more. In fact, she hadn't worked at The Franchise since Friday 19th April.

Robert listened to what Rose was saying. How could he prove that Rose had stolen Marion's watch?

Gladys Rees, Rose's friend, gave evidence next. Gladys was thin and pale. She looked very frightened. But her evidence was the same as her friend's.

Robert did not ask these witnesses any questions. The trial was going to be at the Assizes in Norton in two weeks' time. The Sharpes were given bail. Robert drove the Sharpes back to The Franchise.

'We must thank you, Mr Blair, for all your help,' said Mrs Sharpe.

'If we begin to thank Robert for everything he has done, we will never stop,' Marion said with a smile.

Robert said nothing. But he noticed that Marion had called him Robert, not Mr Blair.

––––

Tuesday and Wednesday passed slowly. Then on Thursday,

something unexpected happened.

When Robert visited The Franchise, Marion had something to show him.

'Look, it's my watch,' Marion said. 'It was sent in the post.'

The watch was in a little box, wrapped in paper. There was a small piece of paper with it. On the paper were the words i DONT WANT NONE of iT. The words were badly written in capital letters.

'Why do you think Rose sent it back?' Marion asked.

'I don't think Rose did send it,' Robert said. 'Rose might have thrown the watch away. But she wouldn't have sent it back.'

'Who did send it then?'

'Gladys Rees. I think Rose gave the watch to Gladys and told her what to say in court. Then Gladys became frightened and sent it back to you. Let me have the piece of paper and the box, please. Now we can prove that these two girls are lying.'

When Robert got back to his office, Alec Ramsden was waiting for him. He looked very unhappy.

'I had to come and see you,' said Ramsden. 'Mr Blair, we're wasting your money. We've checked everywhere. If Betty Kane left the country – and I believe she did – then she looked completely different from the girl in this photograph. She was probably wearing make-up. Perhaps she had her hair pinned on top of her head. That makes a big difference, you know.'

'It is difficult,' Robert said. 'But we must find out where Betty Kane was, all those weeks. You must keep on looking.

'But I've got something to show you,' Robert went on. He took a box from his pocket and said, 'I think Gladys Rees' handwriting is on this piece of paper. Can you prove it?'

'I'm sure I can,' Alec Ramsden said. 'I'll find out where she went to school. There will be an example of her writing in the school.'

'Thank you,' Robert said. 'That will be a great help.'

Robert stood up and walked towards the window.

'I must prove in court that Betty Kane is a liar,' said Robert. 'What chance do you think we have?'

'At the moment, none at all,' Alec Ramsden answered sadly.

But when Ramsden returned the following day, he was looking happy.

'Look at this,' he said to Robert. He put a large piece of paper on the table. It was a map of Canada. It was very carefully drawn. At the bottom was written: DOMiNiON OF CANADA and it was signed: Gladys Rees.

The two men stared at the map.

'Well done,' said Robert. 'There's no doubt the handwriting is the same.'

'I'm going to take the map and the piece of paper to a handwriting expert[35] in London,' Ramsden said.

11

Mr Lange

A week before the trial, a tall, heavy man walked into Robert's office.

'Mr Blair?' he said. 'My name is Lange. I have some information for you. I hope you will find it useful.'

'Sit down, Mr Lange,' Robert said. 'What do you want to tell me?'

'I am Danish, Mr Blair. I have a hotel in Copenhagen, called The Red Shoes. We often have English visitors.'

Suddenly Robert felt very excited.

'Yes, yes, go on, Mr Lange,' he said quickly.

'These English visitors leave English newspapers in their

rooms. Now I am interested in improving my English. So these papers are collected and taken to my office. When I have time, I read them.'

Robert sat very still. Was this the evidence he was looking for?

'So,' Mr Lange went on, 'one day I take this newspaper and look at it.'

Out of his pocket, he took a copy of *The Morning Watch* for Friday 10th May. The face of Betty Kane looked up at them.

'The paper says this is Betty Kane,' Mr Lange went on. 'But it is also the photograph of Mrs Chadwick. She stayed at my hotel with her husband.'

'What!' Robert said excitedly. 'Are you sure?'

'Completely sure. They stayed for two weeks. While this girl says she was starving in an attic, little Mrs Chadwick was eating good Danish food in my hotel!

'At first, I couldn't believe it was the same girl,' Mr Lange went on. 'Most of the time, Mrs Chadwick had her hair pinned up on top of her head. But one night, we had a Fancy Dress Party. And for the party, she wore her hair down. Then she looked just like this photograph. Betty Kane and Mrs Chadwick are the same woman!'

Robert sat back in his chair and smiled.

'Mr Lange,' he said. 'I am extremely delighted that you have come to tell me this. Can you tell me the exact dates this girl stayed with you in Copenhagen?'

'Yes, of course. She and her husband, Bernard Chadwick, arrived by air on Friday 29th March. They left on 15th April.'

'Thank you. And the man, what did he look like?'

'Young. Dark hair. Quite good-looking. He was in Copenhagen on business.'

'What kind of business?'

'This is a photograph of Mrs Chadwick. She stayed at my hotel.'

'I'm sorry, Mr Blair. I don't know. In the hotel register he said he lived in London.'

———

For three days Robert and Alec Ramsden worked harder than they had ever worked before. They phoned every company in London that traded with Denmark. It was Alec Ramsden who found the company that Bernard Chadwick worked for.

Then they talked to all the people who would be needed as witnesses at the trial. On the day before the Assizes, all the evidence was ready.

On Wednesday 5th June, the day before the trial, Robert drove over to The Franchise. He was going to take the Sharpes to Norton, where the Assizes were held.

Marion and Mrs Sharpe were waiting for Robert when he arrived. Robert was now sure that he loved Marion. And he was sure that Marion loved him too. He decided that they would get married as soon as the trial was over.

As Marion shut the door of The Franchise, Robert said, 'The house will be empty tonight. I'll phone Inspector Hallam. He'll send a policeman to guard it.'

'It's an ugly old house,' Marion said with a smile. 'But it is our home. I don't want anything to happen to it.'

'I'll phone the Inspector from Norton,' Robert said again.

But the following morning, the phone rang in Robert's hotel room. Inspector Hallam had bad news.

'The Franchise was burnt down last night,' he said. 'I sent a policeman, but the house was already on fire when he arrived. It's been destroyed.'

'Was anything saved?'

'Yes,' the Inspector replied. 'The firemen managed to get some furniture out before the roof fell in. Thank God the Sharpes weren't there. Will you tell them, Mr Blair, or will I?'

42

'I'll tell them,' Robert said. 'But not until after the trial. Thank you for telling me, Inspector.'

Robert put down the phone. The Franchise was an ugly old house, he thought. He was glad it had burnt down. He would find a better home for Marion.

12

The Trial

There were more than a hundred people in the courtroom at Norton. It was very warm, but everyone sat very still. No one made a sound. Betty Kane was the first witness. She went into the witness box and took the oath. Then the prosecuting counsel[36] asked her to tell her story.

Betty Kane was wearing grey again. She looked sweet and innocent. Robert knew where she had been in those missing weeks. But he still found it hard to believe. What a story it was going to be for the papers!

Betty Kane told the court about the beatings and her stay in the attic. Then the prosecuting counsel sat down.

Then Kevin Macdermott, the defending counsel, stood up to cross-examine her.

'Miss Kane,' he began, 'was it dark when you were taken to The Franchise?'

'Yes, very dark.'

'And the night you escaped. Was it dark then too?'

'Oh, yes, very dark,' Betty Kane said again.

'So you never saw the outside of the house at all?'

'Never.'

'But in your statement,' Kevin said quietly, 'you said that the drive divides into two and makes a circle in front of the door.'

'That's right, it does.'

'How do you know, Miss Kane?'

'Because I saw it from the attic window, later on.'

'My Lord,' Kevin said, turning to the Judge, 'I can bring witnesses who will swear that the circle can't be seen from the attic window.'

Betty Kane said nothing. The look on her face did not change.

'Have you ever been abroad, Miss Kane?' Kevin asked.

'Abroad?' the girl repeated in surprise. 'No, never.'

'So you haven't been to Denmark recently – to Copenhagen?'

'No, of course not.'

'Do you know a man called Bernard Chadwick?' Kevin asked.

Betty Kane stood very still. She was like an animal that could feel danger. But the look on her face did not change.

'No, no, I don't,' she answered.

'Miss Kane,' Kevin said quietly. 'I suggest[37] you spent those missing weeks in an hotel in Copenhagen. I suggest you were never in the attic at The Franchise. Am I wrong?'

'Yes, quite wrong,' Betty Kane answered clearly.

As Kevin Macdermott sat down the prosecuting counsel stood up.

'Miss Kane,' he said, 'you arrived at The Franchise by car, didn't you?'

'Yes.'

'And it was dark. So the headlights of the car showed the curve of the drive?'

'Yes, that's right,' Betty Kane broke in quickly. 'I must have seen the circle then. I told you I'd seen it.'

Rose Glyn was called to the witness box. She repeated her

story. But Kevin Macdermott soon proved that the Sharpes had sacked the girl.

Then Gladys Rees was called to the witness box. She was very frightened. Kevin spoke to her quietly and kindly. Gladys Rees soon told the truth. Rose had given Gladys the stolen watch. She made Gladys promise to agree with her story.

When Bernard Chadwick was called to the witness box, everyone looked at him in surprise. Who was this young man? What had he to do with little Betty Kane?

Bernard Chadwick was married and lived in West London. He told the court that he travelled all over England and often went abroad on business.

'In March this year, did you go to Larborough?' Kevin Macdermott asked.

'Yes,' the young man replied.

'And while you were in Larborough, did you meet Betty Kane?'

'Yes, I did. In the Midland Hotel. She spoke to me and we started talking.'

'She spoke to you first?'

'Yes. She picked me up.'

A sound of surprise went round the court. Good girls like Betty Kane do not pick up young men in hotels!

'Will you tell the Court exactly what happened?' Kevin asked.

'I went to the Midland Hotel for tea one day. Betty Kane was having tea there too.'

'Was she alone?'

'Yes, she was. She smiled at me. I smiled back. Then she spoke. She asked me about my job – things like that.

'Then she suggested we went to the cinema together. I had finished my work, so I said OK. The next day, I met her again. I was driving around on business, so I took her with me. I gave her lunch and tea. She was an amusing kid, so I took her round with me for the next few days. She always went back to her aunt's house in the evening.'

'Did she say anything about her family?'

'Yes. She said she was unhappy at home.'

'And how long did you go on meeting her?'

'Well, we were both leaving Larborough on the same day,' Bernard Chadwick explained. 'She was going back to Aylesbury, to her family. And I was flying to Copenhagen. Then she asked me to take her with me to Copenhagen. She wasn't going back home. She said she was bored there.'

'So you agreed to take Betty Kane to Copenhagen with you?'

'Not at first. She was only sixteen.'

'Is that what she told you?'

'Yes. It was her sixteenth birthday that week. I bought her a lipstick in a gold case.'

'So you did not know that Betty Kane was only fifteen?'

'No, of course not.'

'So you took her abroad – as your wife?'

'Yes.'

'Do you remember the date you left Larborough, Mr Chadwick?' Kevin Macdermott asked.

'Yes, it was 28th March,' Bernard Chadwick answered. 'I met her at the bus stop in the afternoon.'

The court was completely silent. Kevin Macdermott waited a few seconds before asking his next question.

'So you both went to Copenhagen. Where did you stay?'

'At The Red Shoes Hotel. We stayed there for two weeks.'

'And then?'

'We came back to England on 15th April,' Bernard Chadwick went on.

'Did she want to go home then?' asked Kevin Macdermott.

'No,' replied Bernard Chadwick. 'She said she was not going to go home. She was going to write to her family – tell them she had a job!'

13

The Truth

The people in the court began to talk to each other. This man was talking about innocent little Betty Kane! No one could believe it.

But Kevin Macdermott went on with his questions.

'What did you do when you got back to England, Mr Chadwick?' the barrister asked.

'I took Betty Kane down to a cottage I own in the country,' Bernard Chadwick answered.

'Did you stay with her?'

'Yes. I went back to my house in London once. But for the next week, I spent the nights with her. Then one night when I went down, she had gone.'

'Gone?' Kevin repeated.

'Yes. I didn't worry. I thought she was bored. I thought she'd gone somewhere more exciting,' said Chadwick.

'You found out later where she had gone and why?'

'Yes.'

'You heard Betty Kane give evidence today,' Kevin said slowly. 'You heard her say she had been kept in a house in Milford?'

'Yes.'

'And you say that this was the girl who went to Copenhagen with you, Mr Chadwick. Who lived in your cottage in the country?'

'Yes, that is the girl,' Chadwick answered.

'Are you sure?'

'Yes.'

'Thank you.'

Betty Kane's face did not change. It looked as calm, as

innocent as ever.

The prosecuting counsel stood up.

'Mr Chadwick,' he said, 'you must have seen this story in the papers. Why didn't you go to the police?'

'Because I was abroad,' Bernard Chadwick replied. 'I only got back two days ago.'

'I see. But the girl had been badly beaten. Was it you who beat the girl?'

'No, certainly not. I went to the cottage one night and she had gone,' Chadwick said.

'Taking all her things with her?'

'That's what I thought at the time.'

'Thank you, Mr Chadwick,' the barrister said and sat down.

The next witness called by Kevin was a tall, blonde woman. She was Frances Chadwick, Bernard Chadwick's wife. What could she say about the case?

Frances Chadwick had plenty to say.

When her husband returned from Copenhagen, she thought he was seeing another woman. Then someone told her that there was a woman in their cottage in the country.

'Did you ask your husband about her?' Kevin asked.

'No. It's not the first time it's happened. Bernard has had love affairs with other women before. I decided to make her leave.'

'So you went to the cottage?'

'Yes. I went late one evening,' Mrs Chadwick replied. 'I thought I'd catch Bernie there too.

'I had my key. So I opened the door and walked straight in. The girl was on the bed. She was wearing a nightdress and eating chocolates. I pulled her off the bed and hit her hard. She looked so surprised that I laughed. I hit her again and then she started to fight.

'I was bigger and I hit her very hard. She tripped and fell on the floor. She didn't get up. I went into the kitchen to make some

'She was wearing a nightdress and eating chocolates.'

coffee. When I went back to the bedroom with the coffee, she had gone.'

'What did you do then?' Kevin asked.

'I waited for Bernie to come, but he didn't. So I put her things in a suitcase and put the suitcase in a cupboard. I tidied the place up and left.'

'Did you tell your husband what you had done?'

'Yes.'

'Weren't you worried about the girl?'

'No. Bernie told me she could take care of herself. So I forgot all about her.'

'Did you know that this girl was Betty Kane?'

'No, I didn't. Bernie always called the girl Liz. I didn't think it was the same girl.'

'But the girl you saw in the cottage was Betty Kane?'

'Yes, I'm sure of that now.'

Frances Chadwick left the witness box.

The court case was over. Betty Kane's story was proved to be completely untrue. The Sharpes were not guilty.

14

The End of The Franchise Affair

Robert met the Sharpes outside the courtroom.

'Congratulations!' he said. 'It's all over.'

Marion looked at Robert's face and smiled sadly.

'And it is you we must thank,' she said. Then she went on, 'We have heard that The Franchise has burned down.'

'I suppose we'd better go to an hotel,' Mrs Sharpe said.

Robert booked a room for them at the Rose and Crown.

The next morning, Robert and Marion went for a walk together.

'I want you to marry me, Marion. You will, won't you?'

'No, Robert. I won't.'

'But, Marion, why not? I thought . . .'

'Robert, I'm very fond of you,' Marion said quietly. 'But you are a country solicitor. People in Milford will never forget The Franchise Affair.'

'Marion, I don't care what people think!' Robert shouted. 'I'm asking you to be my wife! Don't you care for me?'

'Yes, Robert. I care for you a great deal. But there are many women in Milford who would love to marry you. Why do you choose me?'

'Because you are different from all those other woman and I love you.'

Marion smiled sadly.

'I'm sorry,' she said. 'I can't marry you.'

'What are you going to do?' Robert asked.

'Mother and I are going to live in Canada.'

'To Canada? Why?' said Robert in surprise.

'I have a cousin there.' Marion told him. 'Before we moved to The Franchise, he asked us to go and live with him then. We refused, but we will both be glad to go now.'

'I see.'

'Don't look so sad, Robert. One day you'll be glad I said no,' Marion said. And they walked on in silence.

Three days later, the Sharpes left Milford for the last time. They sold their car and the few pieces of furniture saved from the fire.

Robert drove them to Larborough station. As the London train carried them away, Robert was filled with a great sadness. How could he go on living in Milford without Marion?

Robert had a lot of work to do. Three weeks passed. Then he received a letter from Marion.

My dear Robert,
   This is a short note to say goodbye. We are leaving for Montreal the day after tomorrow. We both send our love to you and our thanks.

Marion

Marion Sharpe

Robert put the letter on his desk. Tomorrow, at this time, Marion would have left England.

———

The passengers for Montreal had all got onto the plane. The plane for Montreal was about to leave. Old Mrs Sharpe and Marion were in their seats. Suddenly Marion looked up and saw Robert.
   'Robert!' she said. 'What are you doing here?'
   'I'm flying to Canada too.'
   'To Canada? But why?'
   'To see my sister,' said Robert, smiling.
   Marion began to laugh.

POINTS
FOR
UNDERSTANDING

Points for Understanding

1

1 Give these facts about Robert Blair:
   (a) his age and his business
   (b) the town he lived in
   (c) how long he had lived there
2 Marion Sharpe phoned Robert Blair.
   (a) What was the name of the house she lived in?
   (b) Why did Marion need the help of a solicitor?
3 Did Marion and her mother have many friends?
4 Why was Detective-Inspector Grant at The Franchise?

2

1 Give these facts about Betty Kane:
   (a) her age and the name of her guardian
   (b) where Betty and her guardian lived
2 Betty went to stay with her aunt in Larborough. What was the name of her aunt?
3 Why did Mrs Wynn write a letter to Betty's aunt?
4 What did Betty's aunt say in her reply to Mrs Wynn?
5 How long had Betty Kane been missing by the time the police were told?
6 Betty Kane had made a statement to the police. What had she said in her statement?
7 What did Robert ask himself when he saw Betty Kane?
8 What did old Mrs Sharpe say when she saw Betty Kane?
9 Betty Kane described many things in The Franchise correctly. Give two examples.

3

1 Robert Blair phoned The Franchise with good news. What was the good news?
2 What did Robert think of Marion Sharpe?
3 What did Robert decide he would do?

4 On Friday morning, Robert had an unpleasant surprise. What was the unpleasant surprise?
5 Could Betty Kane have seen over the walls round The Franchise from a bus?
6 Who was Leslie Wynn?
7 How did Mrs Wynn describe Betty Kane?
8 What was in Betty Kane's pocket when she came home?

4

1 Who was Kevin Macdermott?
2 Who did Kevin think would be believed in court: Betty Kane or the Sharpes?
3 What did Robert learn on his visit to Larborough?

5

1 What did Robert find out about the buses that went by The Franchise?
2 By half past twelve, Robert had visited all the coffee-shops in Larborough. What had he found out?
3 What did Robert learn from Albert, the waiter, in the Midland Hotel?
4 Why was there a policeman standing outside The Franchise?
5 Marion phoned Robert in the middle of the night.
    (a) What had happened at The Franchise?
    (b) Why would Marion Sharpe and her mother not leave The Franchise?

6

1 Kevin Macdermott said Robert needed a private detective. Why?
2 Why had Marion and her mother come into Milford?
3 Why did Robert think there was still hope?

7

1 Detective-Inspector Grant said the police had two pieces of evidence against the Sharpes. What were they?
2 Why was it important that Rose Glyn had told Gladys Rees about the screams before the report in the newspaper?
3 When were the Sharpes to appear in court?

8

1 Why had the Sharpes sacked Rose Glyn?
2 What would happen at the Magistrate's Court?

9

1 What mistake had Betty Kane made in her statement?
2 Would the mistake prove that Betty Kane was lying?
3 What must Robert do before the trial at the Assizes?

10

1 What was Betty Kane wearing in court?
2 Why was Robert sure that Betty Kane was not as innocent as she looked?
3 Marion Sharpe received a parcel by post. It was her watch in a little box wrapped up in paper.
    (a) What was written on the paper?
    (b) Why was Robert sure that it was not Rose who had sent the watch? Who did he think had sent it?
4 How did Alec Ramsden prove that it was Gladys who had sent the watch back to Marion Sharpe?

11

1 Mr Lange's hotel was called The Red Shoes:
    (a) Where was his hotel?
    (b) Why did he read English newspapers?
    (c) What had he seen in *The Morning Watch*?
    (d) How had he known that Mrs Chadwick and Betty Kane were the same person?
2 How did Alec Ramsden find Bernard Chadwick?
3 What did Robert decide he and Marion would do as soon as the trial was over?
4 What happened to The Franchise when the Sharpes were staying in a hotel?

1 Gladys Rees soon told the truth. What was the truth?
2 Why was everyone surprised when Bernard Chadwick was called to the witness box?
3 Why had Bernard Chadwick bought Betty Kane a lipstick in a gold case?
4 How long did Bernard Chadwick and Betty Kane stay in The Red Shoes Hotel?
5 When they got back to England, what did Betty Kane tell Bernard Chadwick she was going to do?

13

1 Where did Bernard Chadwick take Betty Kane?
2 Who found Betty Kane and gave her a beating?
3 How did the court case come to an end?

14

1 Robert asked Marion to marry him. What was her reply?
2 Marion was on a plane going to Canada. Who was on the same plane?

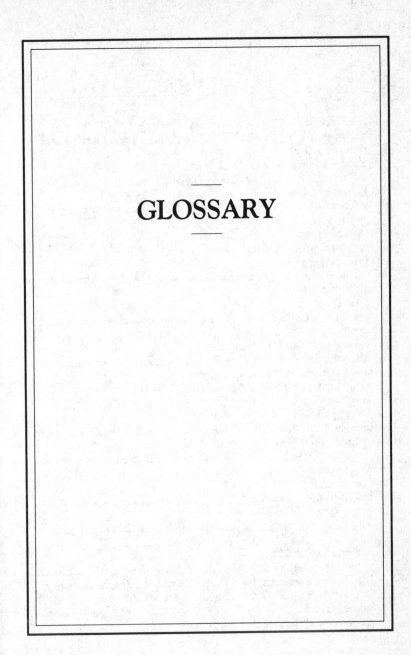

GLOSSARY

Glossary

1 *solicitor* (page 6)
a solicitor is a lawyer who helps people when they get into trouble with the police.

2 *Yard – Scotland Yard* (page 6)
the headquarters of the police in England.

3 *kidnapped* (page 6)
when someone is taken away secretly and kept locked up, they are kidnapped.

4 *starved* (page 8)
not given any food to eat.

5 *bruises* (page 9)
coloured marks left on a person's skin when they have been beaten or hit with a stick.

6 *attic* (page 9)
a small room at the top of a house. The window of an attic is often in the roof.

7 *lift – offer of a lift* (page 10)
when the driver of a car stops and asks someone if they want to be taken somewhere, he is offering them a lift.

8 *exhausted – completely exhausted* (page 10)
very, very tired.

9 *drive* (page 10)
a roadway which leads up to the front door of a large house.

10 *details – check some details* (page 11)
to check the facts that Betty Kane gave in her statement to see if they are correct.

11 *liar* (page 11)
a person who does not tell the truth. A liar is a person who tells lies.

12 *arrest* (page 11)
when the police think that someone has broken the law, they arrest him.

13 *recognise* (page 11)
to look at something and remember that you have seen it before. Old Mrs Sharpe is sure that the girl, Betty Kane, is telling lies. So she is sure that Betty will say she recognises things in the attic.

14 *affair* (page 11)
an event or something that happens.

15 *case* (page 14)
anything which the police think is a crime is called a case.
16 *solve* (page 14)
to find the answer to a problem or to find out who has done
something wrong.
17 *engaged* – *get engaged* (page 16)
when two people agree to get married, they get engaged.
18 *jealous* (page 16)
angry or sad because the person you love loves someone else.
19 *invent* (page 16)
to make up a story which is not true.
20 *memory* – *photographic memory* (page 16)
to be able to look at something for a very short time and remember it
exactly.
21 *barrister* (page 18)
a barrister is a lawyer who speaks in court for a person who has been
arrested (See Glossary no. 12).
22 *opinion* – *to ask someone for their opinion* (page 18)
Robert Blair goes to Kevin Macdermott to ask him what he thinks
should be done to help the Sharpes.
23 *detective* – *private detective* (page 22)
a private detective is a detective who does not work for the
government. People pay a private detective to solve crimes.
24 *guilty* (page 27)
a person who has committed a crime – broken the law – is guilty. A
person who has not committed a crime is innocent.
25 *cleared* – *their name to be cleared* (page 27)
Robert Blair wants to clear the Sharpes' name – he wants everyone to
know that the Sharpes are innocent.
26 *court* – *a summons to appear in court* (page 28)
a summons is an official letter to a person telling them that they must
come to court.
27 *witness* (page 29)
a witness comes to court to say what they know about a crime which
has been committed.
28 *evidence* (page 29)
anything which helps to prove that an accused person is guilty or
innocent is evidence. What a witness says in court is evidence.

29 *assault – charge with abduction and assault* (page 30)

the Sharpes are accused of taking Betty Kane into their house, locking her up and beating her.

30 *sack* (page 30)

to make someone leave their job.

31 *swear* (page 31)

people who give evidence in court must swear that what they say is true. You swear by putting your hand on a holy book and promising to tell the truth.

32 **Court** – *Magistrate's Court* (page 31)

in England, a case is first heard in a Magistrate's Court. The magistrate decides if there is enough evidence (See Glossary no. 28) for the accused person to be sent for trial at the Assizes. If the accused is sent for trial, they may be put in prison until the trial. Or they may be given bail. People who are given bail pay some money, promise to come to court for the trial and are allowed to stay at home.

33 *dock* (page 35)

the place in the court where the witnesses stand.

34 **innocent** – *young and innocent* (page 35)

Betty Kane looks and behaves like a young girl that does not know anything about life.

35 *expert* – *handwriting expert* (page 39)

someone who can say who has written a piece of handwriting.

36 *counsel* – *prosecuting counsel* (page 43)

in a trial at the Assizes, the barrister who tries to prove that the accused person is guilty (See Glossary no. 24) is called the prosecuting counsel. The barrister who tries to prove that the accused person is not guilty is called the defending counsel.

37 *suggest* (page 44)

when a counsel in court wants a witness to agree with him, he begins his sentence with the words: 'I suggest . . .'

Shane *by Jack Schaefer*
Old Mali and the Boy *by D. R. Sherman*
Bristol Murder *by Philip Prowse*
Tales of Goha *by Leslie Caplan*
The Smuggler *by Piers Plowright*
The Pearl *by John Steinbeck*
Things Fall Apart *by Chinua Achebe*
The Woman Who Disappeared *by Philip Prowse*
The Moon is Down *by John Steinbeck*
A Town Like Alice *by Nevil Shute*
The Queen of Death *by John Milne*
Walkabout *by James Vance Marshall*
Meet Me in Istanbul *by Richard Chisholm*
The Great Gatsby *by F. Scott Fitzgerald*
The Space Invaders *by Geoffrey Matthews*
My Cousin Rachel *by Daphne du Maurier*
I'm the King of the Castle *by Susan Hill*
Dracula *by Bram Stoker*
The Sign of Four *by Sir Arthur Conan Doyle*
The Speckled Band and Other Stories *by Sir Arthur Conan Doyle*
The Eye of the Tiger *by Wilbur Smith*
The Queen of Spades and Other Stories *by Aleksandr Pushkin*
The Diamond Hunters *by Wilbur Smith*
When Rain Clouds Gather *by Bessie Head*
Banker *by Dick Francis*
No Longer at Ease *by Chinua Achebe*
The Franchise Affair *by Josephine Tey*
The Case of the Lonely Lady *by John Milne*

For further information on the full selection of
Readers at all five levels in the series, please refer
to the Heinemann Guided Readers catalogue.

Heinemann English Language Teaching
A division of Heinemann Publishers (Oxford) Ltd
Halley Court, Jordan Hill, Oxford OX2 8EJ

OXFORD MADRID ATHENS PARIS FLORENCE PRAGUE
SÃO PAULO CHICAGO MELBOURNE AUCKLAND
SINGAPORE TOKYO GABORONE
JOHANNESBURG PORTSMOUTH (NH) IBADAN

ISBN 0 435 27233 0

© Josephine Tey 1948
First published by Peter Davies Ltd. 1948
This retold version for Heinemann Guided Readers
© Margaret Tarner, 1990, 1992
First published 1990
This edition published 1992

Illustrated by Gay Galsworthy
Typography by Adrian Hodgkins
Cover by Paul Dickenson and Threefold Design
Typeset in 11/12.5 pt Goudy
by Joshua Associates Ltd, Oxford
Printed and bound in Malta by Interprint Limited

95 96 97 10 9 8 7 6 5 4 3